ONE NIGHT STANDARD

ARIA GRACE

SURRENDERED PRESS

CONTENTS

1

CORY

"So you come every year?" I flipped through my notebook, looking for the name of a tool I wanted to ask Jasmine about. "Is it always this exciting?"

Jasmine laughed and swatted at my arm. "You're so adorable."

"I am?" I looked up, holding my finger under the name of the software I'd been searching for. "Why?"

She just shook her head. "That's why."

I didn't know what she meant but I didn't care if she was making fun of me. I'd only been in town for ten hours and it was already the best day of my life. Okay, that was overstating things a bit but not by much. From the moment I walked into the convention center, my mind was spinning with ideas and possibilities. The energy in the building was almost palpable as startups and the big names all mingled together to share best practices and advance the industry. Every workshop I attended and every lecture I sat in filled me with plans for what I could be doing better at work and what would impress my boss. "But seriously, this Plan Daddy Xpres looks perfect for what we're doing. I think we should at least do the trial."

She shrugged. "Yeah, I guess."

I grabbed my beer and downed the half that was left in a few gulps. "I'm gonna get another. You want a refill?"

She picked up her phone and started pushing buttons. "Nah, I'm still working on this one."

Jasmine was a few years younger than me but was a lot of fun to hang out with. At least, she usually was. Tonight, she seemed distracted and exhausted. I guess she wasn't on the same conference high I was on. I didn't understand how that was possible. I was buzzing with energy as I hopped up and practically glided to the bar.

The guy pouring drinks stopped what he was doing and gave me a bright smile, as if he were happy to see me. "Hey there. What can I get you?"

I held up my empty glass. "Just another IPA, please."

He nodded toward Jasmine as he filled a fresh pint glass. "What about your girlfriend? Does she want another glass of Cab?"

"Nah, she's not done." I slid my card across the bar as he slid the glass toward me. "And she's not my girlfriend."

His eyes moved from Jasmine to me. "She's pretty. Are you trying to make her your girlfriend?"

"Uh, not really. I mean, she is pretty." I took a sip of my beer and looked back at the woman I'd been working beside for the past six months. "But we work together."

He chuckled. "Even better. Friends with benefits and all that…"

"I am kinda amped up." A quick fling didn't sound bad. It wasn't normally my thing but the few that I'd had were always with women. I turned back to the bartender who was more my type but not someone I would ever consider approaching. "Yeah, maybe I should go for it."

He nodded approvingly as he gave me my card back with the receipt to sign. "I think you should."

With my shoulders pulled back and my chest puffed out, I approached the table. As I sat down, I scooted my chair a little closer to Jasmine's. "So, you're not seeing anyone right now, are you?"

She looked up from her phone with a quizzical expression. "No, why?"

I tapped the side of my glass, making little circles in the condensation so I could avoid looking right at her. "I was just thinking maybe you'd want to go back to my room with me?" I glanced up just to gauge her reaction. "We can have a drink up there where it's a little more comfortable."

Her jaw dropped open as if she had something to say then she closed it and leaned back in the chair. "Thanks, Cory, but I don't think that's a good idea."

Now I just felt stupid, wishing there was a way I could take back my stupid suggestion. "Yeah, of course. You're totally right." I grabbed a cube of cheese off the board we'd been sharing, hoping to change the subject without being obvious about it. "So, what did you think of the Keynote this morning?"

She took a deep pull from her glass then set it on the table between us. "It was good. I need to do more of that mindfulness stuff."

"I wrote down the promo code for their app." Flipping through my notebook again, I searched for the code I'd scribbled down with all my other notes. "I'll send it to you."

"Yeah, sure. Thanks." She smiled then pushed back from the table. "I'm gonna head up. You gonna hang out for a while longer?"

I stood up too, desperate to keep her around a little longer. "Already? Are you sure? Maybe we can go for a walk or something? I'm not ready to sleep."

She cocked her head and gave me a sad look, like she felt sorry for me. It was actually humiliating. "I'm beat. I need to sleep."

I exhaled heavily and nodded. "Okay, well, have a good night. I'll meet you at breakfast tomorrow."

She gave me a half hug and kissed my cheek. "Good night, Cory."

I watched as she walked away then I headed toward the bar. With my glass in hand, I slipped onto an empty stool and looked at the bartender. "I think I need something that'll put me to sleep."

2

——

LANE

I didn't think he'd actually go for it, but when I saw the poor guy's excited smile drop and a flush of shame shine on him like a beacon, I knew he had gone for it...and it didn't end well.

"Shit," I whispered under my breath. Now I felt bad for encouraging him to go for it with his colleague. That was probably a bad idea to begin with, but at least if they were both into it, there would have been a silver lining. Now things would just be awkward for him at work.

I kept my eyes averted so he didn't notice I was watching him, but when the woman got up and left, it was hard to not want to reach out to him. He looked like a lost puppy. And as a bartender, it was practically my duty to make him feel better and forget his woes.

Then he came to my counter and slid right onto the stool in front of me, looking absolutely broken. He asked for a refill of his beer, but he needed something stronger than that. Something that would turn off any shame he might be feeling and help him get past the awkward moment he'd just experienced.

"How about I buy you a shot?" I pulled two shot glasses off the rack and set them directly in front of him. "I'll even do one with you."

"A shot?" It looked like he'd never had hard liquor before in his life.

"Whiskey or scotch?" I lifted up both bottles and held them so he could choose. "We're just about to close up for the night, so yeah, let's do this."

Once again, his eyes were wide in a mix of shock and fear...and maybe even a little bit of something else. "Okay, whiskey, I guess."

I nodded approvingly as I put the scotch bottle down and poured the top shelf whiskey into the glasses. This ritual was pretty much how I ended every shift, so it wasn't anything new for me. But when the guy took a whiff of the liquid and had to hold back a gag, I knew it probably wasn't a regular drink for him. "On the count of three?"

He swallowed hard and then nodded as he held the glass just below his chin and stared at me.

I did the same, locking my gaze with his as I slowly counted. "One. Two." I held up my glass for the third count and pressed it to my mouth, sucking down the full contents with ease.

He took a deep breath then swallowed the whiskey without even coughing any of it up. I could tell by the faces he was making he didn't like it, but he was able to get it down. "Nice. Want another?" I was only half teasing because I knew he wouldn't want any more.

He pushed the glass away from him and made a face. "No, thanks. I think I've had enough."

Grabbing both empty glasses, I nodded and turned to the sink to rinse them out before putting them in the washer. "So, she didn't go for it?"

"No. I don't know what I was thinking." He scoffed as he rested his forehead on his open palm. "There's no way she would be interested in me. And she's definitely not my type."

"Not your type?" I raised an eyebrow, questioning his sanity. "We already established she's beautiful. So if that's not your type, what is?" In the back of my mind, I had a feeling about what his real answer was, but I wasn't sure what he would say to me. I decided to give him a nudge. "Because if I were into women, I think she'd be my type."

Once again, this poor guy was shocked silent. Maybe because he'd never met a gay man before or maybe he'd just never heard one speak so openly about it. Either way, I didn't want to make him more uncomfortable than he already was, so I merely winked and walked to the end of the bar to grab some empty glasses that were waiting there, giving him some space to think.

Or walk away from me forever.

After several long minutes went by, I finally heard his voice again. "Yeah. Me too."

I really wasn't sure what he was talking about, so I looked up. "You too, what?"

He turned and inspected the area around him before responding. In a soft voice, he reminded me of what I'd last said. "If I were into women, she'd probably be my type too."

"Oh, shit. I didn't realize…" Now it was my turn to be shocked into silence. "I hope I didn't encourage you to do something you weren't comfortable doing." Thank god she said no. If I had pushed him into a hook up with a woman that he wasn't interested in, I'd feel terrible.

"No, no." He shrugged and looked at his fingers, laced together on the bar in front of him. "I usually date women. It's just…easier that way."

Huh. There were a lot of ways I could approach this situation, but my stiffening dick had a plan of his own. I leaned forward in front of my new friend and rested my elbows on the bar. "That doesn't sound easier to me."

His tongue darted out of his mouth and slowly slid across his bottom lip, then back over his top, wetting it as if he were about to kiss me. Of course, he wasn't.

He was getting ready to confide in me. "I've never actually been with a man, but I think that's what I prefer."

Damn. I didn't quite know how to respond to that. Ass virgins were sexy as hell, but I wasn't sure he was up for anything after his recent rejection. So I went with light and flirty, my speciality. "Well, I have and it's pretty easy."

"Oh." He looked like he might melt right into the stool, though I wasn't sure which emotion was burning a crimson tint into his neck and ears. "That's cool."

"So, how about I get you a Coke and you wait for me to get closed up..." I reached across the counter and placed two fingers on his joined hands. "And then we can go up to your room?"

3

———

CORY

Was this really happening? I'd never had a hook up quite this casual before, but the more shocking part was that it was with a man. But maybe this was for the best. I could finally pursue my true self, away from my hometown and without any expectations. I nodded. "Um, yeah. That sounds great."

He turned around and reached for a glass before filling it up with Coke from a hose. "I think so too."

And then something occurred to me. "I don't even know your name."

He cocked his head to the side as if I was starting to push it too far. Maybe he didn't like to give it out.

Maybe casual meant staying strangers to him. But he must have been feeling generous because he decided to indulge me. "I'm Lane."

"Nice to meet you, Lane. I'm Cory."

I pretended to glance through my brochures while Lane closed out the last few guests and prepared to leave. It didn't take long, or maybe it did and I just felt like time was flying by because my nerves were on overdrive.

But he was suddenly standing in front of me with his jacket over his arm and a sexy grin on his face. "You ready to leave, Cory?"

"Yeah, sure." I stood up and smoothed out the front of my slacks, casually adjusting my dick so it wasn't so obvious I was excited by his presence. "Let's go."

He waved his arm out for me to take the lead. It was a sweet gesture that made me smile, momentarily forgetting how nervous I was.

I felt like rocks were bouncing around in my stomach as we crossed the lobby together and stopped at the elevator. "I'm on five."

"Relax, Cory. I don't bite." He placed his hand on my shoulder and gave me a gentle squeeze. "At least not until I know you want me to."

I sucked in a deep breath as the doors opened to an empty elevator. I was partially relieved no one else was in there, but as soon as the doors closed, confining us in the tight space together, the magnitude of what we were about to do hit me. "Do you do this every night?"

It wasn't any of my business but the thought struck me and I couldn't shake it.

"Yes, most nights." Lane leaned against the wall of the car for just a second then pushed off as the doors opened on the fifth floor. "Does that bother you?"

I shrugged, not sure how I felt about any of it. "No. I'm just wondering."

He nodded and waved his arm for me to exit the car but he didn't get out with me. He just held the doors open with one hand. "Are you sure you want to do this? It's okay if you don't."

"I do." I really did. Like, really badly. I was just scared I'd do it wrong. "Just first time nerves, I guess."

He watched me for a few long seconds and I was sure he was about to take the elevator back down to the lobby and go find some other hookup for the night. And that made me sad. If he was going to have a one-night stand tonight, and he was willing to have it with me, I wasn't going to let the opportunity pass without at least trying to make it work. He was way out of my league for anything serious, but for a quickie during a business trip, he seemed willing to make it work. As long as I was willing to put forth some effort too.

I reached out for his hand, hoping he'd take it. "At least hit the mini bar with me for a little bit. We can take it from there."

A slow and sexy grin covered his face. "You are pretty cute when you drink." He stepped out and let the elevator doors close behind him. "Your cheeks get a little rosy, and you talk with your hands a lot."

I could feel my face heating up again as we walked down the hall toward my room. "I get the hand thing from my mom. The cheeks…" I shrugged. "I think that's a combination of a few things."

"Oh yeah?" He stepped closer to my side and his arm wound around my back before resting on my shoulder. "What kind of things?"

He was gonna make me say the words, wasn't he? "Embarrassment. Anxiety." I glanced at him from under my lashes then stopped in front of room 525. "Lust…"

Lane closed his eyes and rested his head against the door frame as I pulled my room key from my wallet. "You're killing me, Cory."

The rocks in my belly started to settle and my nerves began to shift closer toward excitement. I wanted to spend the night with Lane. A man. The kind of man who could show me what I'd been missing all those years and help me accept my reality. "Well, then, let's get this party started."

4

—

LANE

Cory was adorably nerdy, especially when he was trying to flirt. And to my surprise, I found that refreshing. Most of the guys I hooked up with were card-carrying playboys who didn't give a shit about impressing me or learning my name. And that was a good thing because I didn't ever want anything from them either. I was managing the bar and on a growth path to potentially head up a new casino bar in Vegas if things stayed good with the chain I was working for. Falling for a stranger was totally unrealistic, especially given our vastly different career paths.

He was a techy guy who got off on reading brochures about apps and circuit boards or whatever the hell those things are called. Personally, I hated computers. I used them because they were basically a requirement of the job but I liked to be off technology as often as possible. It was the Boy Scout in me who preferred to be creating stuff with my hands rather than just my fingers. That's part of the reason I became a bartender. I loved playing with recipes, serving my customers, and getting to know people from all over the world. The fact that I was able to get to know some of them in a more biblical sense was just frosting on the cake of my life.

But a guy like Cory needed more than a smooth talker. He needed someone to be gentle and patient with him. It was his first time and I wanted him to look back on this night with fond memories, not shame or disappointment. So, I turned on my charm and decided to up my foreplay game by actually putting some effort into seducing him. He still had all the control and could stop things at any moment. I just hoped like fuck he wouldn't.

"Looks like you've got just about everything in here..." I pulled out the wooden tray that held single shot servings of all the most popular liquor. "If there's still a cranberry bottle in the fridge, do you want a vodka cran?"

He nodded vigorously as if that was the segue he'd been waiting for. It was cute how nervous and excited he could be at the same time. It's like a kid in line for a roller coaster. They know they want to ride it, but they're also afraid of puking. That's what Cory looked like.

After preparing a couple drinks, I walked to the king-sized bed and took a seat on the side that faced the window so we could look out at the city lights. Cory didn't follow me immediately but after a few seconds, he came and sat beside me, his thigh pressed tightly against mine.

"Here ya go." I handed him one glass then positioned mine between us to toast his. "To a fun night with a new friend."

His eyes flicked to mine and he held my gaze as he clinked his glass against mine. "Cheers."

For the next several minutes, we just sat there and sipped our drinks, looking out the window at the excitement of the city surrounding us. But he must have felt some pressure to make a move because Cory abruptly put his drink on the nightstand then turned his body slightly to face me. "How do we start?"

I threw back the rest of my drink in a single gulp then put my glass down on the floor. I turned to Cory and looked right in his eyes, slowly letting the moment sink in for him. "We can start with a kiss, if that's okay with you."

His tongue instinctively slid across his lower lip and then his upper lip, moistening it before I made contact. Cory nodded and leaned slightly forward before letting his eyelids drift shut.

My hand had been resting on his thigh so it slid up to his hip and then around to his back so I could hold him steady as my mouth gently pressed against his. I just held my skin on his for a moment before closing my lips over his lower lip and pulling away.

Cory's eyes immediately popped open and instead of waiting for me to kiss him again, he flung his whole body at me, pressing me against the mattress as he lay his full weight on my chest. His mouth was hungry as it sought to learn my skin, my textures, my limits.

He didn't know I had no limits so I just relaxed and let him explore. His tongue tentatively tasted my lips before slipping between them and making contact with my tongue. The warmth of his personality extended all the way to the tip of his tongue as he tested and teased my mouth before kissing the corner of my lips. A small moan escaped my lungs as I let his inexperience guide the encounter.

I wanted Cory to learn my body.

To feel my reactions.

To react to me too.

And based on the painful rod digging into my thigh, he was just as influenced by me as I was by him.

5

———

CORY

I don't know where my sudden inhibition and dominance came from, but I was grateful for it. If I had continued to just stare stupidly out the windows, Lane would have surely taken off, convinced I wasn't interested in him.

That was about as far from the truth as one could get.

It took all my strength not to dry hump his leg and come right in my slacks once we started kissing. He was a gentle giant, ceding control to me while I found the courage to move forward. It was empowering to know a man like Lane would let me use his body for my own pleasure, enjoying him the way my instincts directed despite not having any practical experience.

In fact, he pulled a pillow from the head of the bed and slipped it behind his neck so he could sit back and watch as I kissed down the front of his shirt before yanking it up and over his head. He smiled, somewhat amused by my sudden burst of confidence. "That feels nice."

I glanced up from his chest, my lips closed around the tip of his nipple before my teeth teasingly nipped at him. "Yeah?"

Lane's fingers slipped through my hair and he made a loose fist, gently pulling the hairs for a second in the most erotic way. The little spikes of pain seemed to shoot straight to my dick and it filled up even thicker. "I wonder what else you'd be good at sucking."

My confidence started to waver as I contemplated his words. He wanted me to suck his dick. And don't get me wrong, I wanted to suck his dick. Badly. I was just afraid of doing it...badly. "Will you tell me how?"

His eyes softened as he looked at me. "I will if you need help, but I think you'll figure it out."

I swallowed hard even though my throat was suddenly dry then dragged my tongue down to the button of his pants. For a brief second, I considered trying to open his button and zipper with my teeth, but I didn't chance it. With my luck, I'd break a tooth and cut off his dick with a jagged bite.

So I stood up and then lowered myself to my knees between Lane's legs.

He sat up, watching me carefully as I released the front of his pants and then leaned back to give him space to remove them. Lane moved just an inch off the mattress so he could slide his pants and boxers down then sat back, allowing me some time to take in the view.

I'd seen plenty of dicks in porn and locker rooms. Some even close up when no one was paying attention to me in the gym showers. But I'd never been close enough to touch one. And I'd never seen one as perfectly shaped and proportioned as Lane's. Much like his thick muscles and wide shoulders, his cock was a monster with veins and ridges that just begged to be licked.

My fear of disappointing him evaporated as soon as I saw the kind encouragement in his eyes. He wasn't pressuring me and he wasn't being greedy. He wanted me to take as much as I wanted, and I could tell he knew this was something I wanted.

Taking a deep breath, I leaned forward and pressed my puckered lips against his glans, moistening my mouth with the drop of liquid that had settled there. Without thinking about how Lane might feel about it, I licked my lips, tasting a man's come for the first time ever.

It was heavenly.

The time for hesitation had passed, and I was ready to dive right in. With my mouth open wide, I sucked the head of his cock through my lips until it was resting on my tongue. I wasn't sure how deep I could get him, but I had a long tongue and was able to stick it out in almost a taco shape to create a warm, wet slide for him to drag forward and backward on. When he pushed deep enough to hit the back of my throat, I gagged for an instant, but I didn't let him stop.

My fingers dug into his hard ass muscles, holding him in place while I moved his dick in and out of me.

"Fuck, Cory. I thought you said you'd never done this before..." He threw his head back and looked up at the ceiling as I pressed him in even deeper.

I tried to answer him but with my mouth full of dick, it just came out as a jumbled mess of moaning and humming sounds.

Lane gasped and his big palm held the back of my head in place as a flood of cream shot down my throat.

I swallowed as much as I could but I wasn't expecting him to come right then so several large drops escaped the corners of my mouth. Not sure how to handle the situation, I used my hand to capture the gobs of seed before they dripped onto the comforter.

Before I could do anything with it, Lane reached for my hand and pulled me up to stand. For a second, I was afraid he was going to get up and leave, but he quickly shifted our positions so I was on my back and he was standing above me.

He held my hand to his face then licked up the come I'd gathered. Then he leaned down and kissed me on the mouth, transferring his seed from his tongue to mine so I could drink it all.

It was the sexiest move I could have possibly experienced, and my balls were starting to ache from the desperate need to explode. While he kissed me hard and fast, I slipped a hand between us and opened up my slacks to get to my cock.

Just a few firm strokes, and I'd catch up to him, blowing a heavy load between us as a sexy man with tattoos covering much of his arms and torso kissed me like there was no tomorrow.

6

———

LANE

THE SHY MAN I SAW IN THE ELEVATOR WAS GONE and I didn't think he'd ever be back. The man beneath me, kissing me with a passion so hot there were practically sparks between us, was like an uncaged animal, finally escaping the walls he'd been surrounded by and running free for the first time ever.

I loved it.

And I wanted more.

In fact, I was so caught up in the softness of his lips and the teasing of his tongue that I almost missed the fact that Cory had pulled out his dick and was getting ready to come.

That wouldn't do. Not yet anyway. He was probably good for a few orgasms before needing to rest but I wanted the first one to be amazing. The first time he came with a man should be mind blowing and relaxing, not from jacking off like some kid in the shower.

I lifted my weight off him and stilled his hand with mine. "May I?"

Cory nodded and let his arm fall to the mattress as he lay back, watching to see what I'd do next.

Before getting him off, I wanted to get him ready for the rest of my plans so I carefully undressed him until he was on display in front of me with a hard dick standing straight in the air. His cock was long and lean, and my mouth watered just looking at it. I wanted to taste him but I didn't want him to come in my mouth. Not until he let me fuck him. At least, if he wanted to fuck.

He was definitely giving out a "Put your dick in me" vibe, but I wasn't sure if that was left over from when he was sucking my cock. To test the waters, I bent down and kissed the length of his shaft while spreading his legs with one hand.

Cory whimpered softly and his hand closed on my head. If my hair were long enough to grab, he would have. But he settled for palming me like a basketball with slight pressure, just enough to let me know he wanted more of what I was doing.

Smiling against his smooth skin, I licked up from his base to his tip before sucking his dick into my mouth. While he was distracted, my fingers slid to his opening, gently tapping at his hole to see his reaction.

I half-expected Cory to panic and call the whole thing off, but to my surprise, he pulled both knees back toward his armpits, giving me full access to his tight rosebud.

Wanting to reward him for his generosity and trust, I gave him a few long thrusts, sucking his dick fully into my throat before releasing his head and kissing down his balls until my tongue was as his opening.

With Cory's legs spread open, I took a minute to capture a mental picture of his virgin hole before I licked the soft skin. Gently pressing, I worked him open with my pointed tongue and slowly fucked his hole a few times before attempting a finger. "Are you doing okay?"

He pulled in a deep breath and exhaled. "Yeah, but I want to come. Please."

I reconsidered my strategy to make him wait but then decided to stick with my plan. We would both enjoy it a lot more if there was some penetration. "Have you ever played with your ass before? Toys or your fingers?"

He closed his eyes and nodded. "My fingers. But you're much better at it."

I grinned and reached for my pants on the floor. I had a few condoms in my pocket and some small packets of lube. I never leave home unprepared. "If you think that's good, just wait until I really get started."

"I will." He watched as I rolled on the condom and then covered the latex with boy butter.

I could tell he was as curious about everything I was doing as he was turned on. His cock didn't soften at all and by the time I was ready to slip a buttered up finger into him, he was leaking precome in small pools on his belly. "Tell me if it hurts or you need a break."

Cory exhaled deeply and his whole body relaxed, including the muscles that I was trying to get past with my index finger.

I teased his balls with my tongue, tracing the sac while I slowly pressed my finger all the way inside. He didn't flinch or wince at all, so I wasn't sure he even felt me. "Are you okay?"

He smiled. "I want more."

More was something I could do. As long as we were just talking about tonight, I could give him as much *more* as he wanted.

7

———

CORY

My heart was pounding in my chest and I wasn't sure I'd survive the anticipation as he shoved me back on the mattress and settled on the bed between my legs. My knees were pulled back and I watched closely as he continued to open me up, loosening my muscles so he could fit his huge cock inside me.

I didn't think it was possible for him to fit inside me, but I wanted nothing more than for him to try. I could be tough when I wanted something and I wanted this badly. I wanted to feel him breaching my opening for the first time and giving me something I never thought I'd get. Something I never believed I'd ever have the guts to go through with.

Lane reached up and brushed a few strands of hair off my forehead then his thumb brushed across my lower lip. "You doing alright?"

I exhaled and smiled. "Yeah, just... it's a lot."

"Are you hurting?" His expression changed completely and his fingers stopped. "I can stop."

"No, don't stop. I love it. I'm just..." My eyes pricked like maybe they'd tear up and I didn't want him to think I was crying. I wasn't. I was relieved and excited. And apparently, that made me a bit emotional. "So damn happy to be here. With you."

He leaned forward and kissed me, softer this time, as he pulled his hand away. "I think you're ready. Do you think you're ready?"

My heels dug into the bed and my ass lifted up until I felt the head of his lubed up cock touch my hole. "I'm ready."

His eyes were locked on mine as he pushed forward, slowly entering my body with measured control. He'd definitely done this before.

But that wasn't what was going through my mind as the sting set in. What I was thinking about as he filled me so completely that I thought I might not be able to take another breath, was that I was important to him. He cared about making this good for me. His gentleness was for me. His slow movements were for me.

And when he was as deep as he could get, and his warm balls rested on my ass, I knew I could never go back to pretending. I could never go back to dating women because it was easier. I needed this connection. I needed a man like Lane to look at me like I was the most important person in his world. It might not have been true, but no one had ever made me even consider this level of fulfillment was possible.

We were just having sex. And I wasn't just having my ass cherry popped.

I was finally becoming the man I was meant to be. And Lane was the perfect man to share that with. "Keep going."

He nodded once then slowly pulled out to the tip before sliding back inside me. It wasn't a fast motion but it wasn't as slow as before. And within a few strokes, he moved at a faster clip, thrusting deep and then leaving me empty in a steady rhythm that had every synapse firing within my body until I thought I might spontaneously combust. A flood of heat filled me as sensations I'd never experienced before brought me closer to release.

I'd already been on the verge of coming before he started, but once he stimulated me in a new way that I couldn't have even comprehended before, it was a second by second struggle to hold back the rush I was feeling. "I can't hold back much longer."

"You don't have to." Lane thrust faster and reached between us, grabbing my dick in his firm hand and stroking me to the same rhythm. "I'm close too."

I wasn't sure what the etiquette was and if I was supposed to wait for him or not, but I couldn't do it. I couldn't deny the ecstasy that I knew was so closely within reach. I forced out a harsh breath and bared down on him, taking him even deeper as I let the sting and pleasure commingle in a powerful orgasm that took my breath away.

I literally couldn't breathe as my body shook and rocked while my balls emptied between his fingers.

Lane lifted me even higher and held my ass in the air as his body held me in place, his cock fully buried inside me as a low roar escaped from his throat. "Fuck, Cory."

I couldn't speak or even think. Once I was able to gain enough control of my quivering body to inhale a breath, everything else turned to jello. Every ounce of energy went into that climax and I felt like I'd melted into a puddle in the middle of the bed. "Mmm…"

Lane lowered my lower half and stepped away from me for a few seconds. It was a few seconds too long, but he quickly returned and lowered himself onto the bed beside me. "You okay? You're looking a little…tired."

"That's one way to describe it." I smiled and rested my head on his chest. "Completely and utterly spent is another."

He chuckled then put his hand on mine. "Yeah, that was pretty epic. Especially for your first time."

I wanted to ask what he meant by that, but I just didn't have the energy to talk. My mind was having a full conversation with Lane about his life and interests and if he wanted to have dinner tomorrow night, but my eyes drifted shut and I zoned out until I was deep asleep, reliving the best moment of my life in a dream I hoped would become a recurring fantasy because I never wanted to forget even a moment of what we'd just shared.

8
___

LANE

Cory was asleep on my chest within minutes. Between the alcohol in his system and the endorphins flooding through his bloodstream, he had no chance. I watched him sleep for almost thirty minutes before I forced myself to get up. I didn't want to leave without saying goodbye but he was out cold, and he probably had to be up early in the morning for his conference. I had no idea what time but I didn't see him set an alarm so after I carefully slipped out from under his arm and pulled up the comforter from the opposite side of the bed and covered him with it, I set the nightstand clock to six AM then headed out.

This was all standard protocol for me. I met someone. I had a good time with him. And then I left. No fuss and no attachments. Cory might remember me as a good time on a business trip, and as his first time with a man, it might always hold a place in his mind, but I would probably forget about him in a few weeks...maybe a month. I always did. I wasn't the sentimental type, and even though I had a great time with Cory—better than usual—he was just another one-night stand.

A stranger to keep my needs sated while protecting my heart.

A means to an end.

And since I'd likely never see him again, it was easy to chalk up the connection I felt toward him as just good ol' fashioned lust and nothing more. Even though there was a niggling in the back of my brain that kept telling me it was more. It was a lot more. Like when I was with Jake.

I rolled my eyes at myself for allowing that name to even enter my mind space. I hadn't thought about him in years and usually only around Christmas. That was usually the time of year when my fierce independence morphed into stark loneliness and thoughts of "what might have been" started to encroach on my nights.

Regardless, Cory wasn't like Jake. I had been in love with Jake. I thought we were going to spend our lives together. Cory was a stranger who was only in town for a conference. I didn't know where he lived, but it was probably thousands of miles away and I'd never see him again.

At least that's what I told myself as I walked home to my apartment.

THE NEXT NIGHT, Jaxon was working with me behind the bar while a few servers walked the floor. He usually closed up the bar with me, but he'd been feeling sick the night before when I was working alone. And there wasn't much of a crowd.

Tonight, on the other hand, the conference was hosting a long happy hour for attendees and the place was packed.

As much as I tried not to, I kept scanning the room for Cory. Since I didn't do repeat performances, I hoped he wouldn't show up. I didn't want to hurt his feelings if he wanted to get together again, but that didn't stop me from watching out for him during every spare moment. Which, albeit, wasn't a lot.

The company sponsoring the party had requested three signature cocktails, and each drink had at least five ingredients. They weren't complicated, but they took longer than a standard Jack and Coke or vodka soda. Jaxon and I were slammed from the time people started arriving at 5:30 until the hosted portion of the party ended at 9:00.

I'd been on the lookout for Cory or his friend, but it wasn't until the crowd thinned out that I noticed him sitting in a booth at the back of the bar with his laptop in front of him. He had an empty beer mug in front of him, so one of the servers must have gotten it for him because he didn't get it from me or Jaxon.

As if he could feel my stare, he looked up and smiled.

Shit. I didn't want to lead him on so I just turned away, pretending not to notice him even though it was very obvious I did. I turned to a customer that had just walked in and kept my eyes averted from the back of the room.

When two guys I knew from the catering department walked in and took a seat at the bar, I was grateful for the distraction. Jaxon had dated both of these guys but they were just friends to me. I was careful not to hookup with co-workers because it was too hard to stick to my protocol of no repeats. And too awkward to deal with if feelings were hurt.

Colby was holding two potted plants and pushed both across the counter. "I brought you guys a present."

Jaxon lifted up one of the succulents then put it back down. "Why?"

Steve laughed as he pointed to the bottle of Apple Crown Royal on the shelf behind me. "I told you they wouldn't want them."

Colby ignored his friend and turned to Jaxon. "They were part of the decorations for a meeting earlier and they're gonna be thrown away. I can't bear to see them end up in the trash. They're so cute."

Jaxon raised his eyebrows then backed away. "Thanks, man, but I have a rule about no living things in my apartment except me. I can barely keep myself fed and watered. I don't need to kill anything else."

I opened my mouth to ask about the kitten he rescued last summer but decided I probably didn't want to know what had happened to it. "Yeah, I'm not great with plants either."

Colby must have realized Jaxon wasn't exactly the nurturing type because he shoved both pots in my direction. "Come on, Lane. They'll brighten up your place and they're easy to take care of. Just drop an ice cube in the dirt every week or two and they'll be fine."

"Seriously?" I pulled both plants closer to get a better look. "Don't you guys want them?"

Steve shook his head and lifted up his palms. "I sure as hell don't."

Colby sighed. "My mom said I need to stop bringing home strays. I think plants are included in that general sentiment."

Colby was twenty-five but he still lived at home because his parents had a huge house in the Sunset district and with rents as crazy as they were in the city, it didn't make sense for him to put half his paycheck into a shitty apartment when he could live in luxury for free.

Not wanting to seem ungrateful, I grabbed the plants and put them under the counter. "Okay, thanks. I'll put them on the balcony. Tony will probably feel sorry for them and keep them watered."

Steve put his arm on the bar and rested his chin on his fist. "If you put me on the balcony, will Tony water me?"

I rolled my eyes and turned away from the group. A customer was waiting on the other side and I didn't like being rude. Out of habit, I glanced toward the table Cory was at and realized he was gone. He must have left while I was engrossed in plant talk with the guys.

That was a good thing. He took my hint and didn't make a scene. I appreciated that in a hookup. No promises were made and no feelings were hurt.

Although there was a sudden unease roiling in my gut. It wasn't a feeling, per se, and I couldn't describe it as hurting...but a tension overcame me that made me want to chase after him to see if he was okay. It was silly and unprecedented...but I didn't have any other words to describe it.

Dammit, it was a feeling...and it did hurt.

9
___

CORY

When I got to the bar and saw how busy Lane was, I thought I was being polite by staying out of his way and waiting for him to come up for air. I didn't realize it would take two hours for the place to finally empty out enough for him to have a clear line of sight to me. But when I felt his stare on me and looked up, a sudden warmth filled my soul and I was about to stand up to go say hi.

Then he turned away as if he didn't recognize me. Like I was just another stranger amid a room full of strangers that he didn't make passionate love to the night before.

And like a freight train, it hit me.

I was just a stranger among other strangers. I wasn't anyone special or important, despite the way he'd made me feel when he was kissing me and making love to me. No, I needed to stop using that term. He hadn't made love to me. Strangers didn't make love. They fucked.

We fucked.

Nothing more than that. He was a great memory I'd have for the rest of my life, but that was all I'd be taking home with me from this trip. I wanted to hate him. I was tempted to march over to that bar and punch him right in the face. But he didn't do anything wrong. He hadn't made any promise to me. In fact, he didn't even want to tell me his name. That should have been a red flag. It was a red flag at the time but I ignored it because I wanted him so badly. I wanted him to be the man to teach me how to be with another man.

And he did that. Expertly.

I should be grateful. I was grateful.

And the tears pricking at the back of my eyes weren't from anger or embarrassment. At least I didn't think that's where they were coming from. They were from acceptance that the best night of my life had already passed and I'd probably never experience anything like that again. I'd never have a real chance with a man like Lane.

I glanced in his direction and saw that he was talking to a couple guys at the bar, smiling and joking around about some plants.

He'd already moved on and I needed to give him that. I'd gotten what I wanted from him and there was no other reason for me to bother him. I quickly shoved my computer and notepad into my bag then slipped out the back door of the bar, the one that opened to the street instead of the hotel lobby.

This was officially the best and the worst conference of my life.

INSTEAD OF HEADING to my room, I wandered around San Francisco for a few hours. I hadn't had a chance to explore so I ended up at the wharf and just walked up and down the piers, window shopping and trying to distract myself from the ache in my chest.

Being heartbroken was stupid. I'd had plenty of one-night stands with women in the past, and I never thought twice about them. When we parted ways, I knew it was forever, and never once had I felt sadness or regret about that. It was just the way things were and the way I thought they'd always be.

Until I met Lane.

I wished I could go back in time and not agree to bringing him back to my room, but then quickly dismissed that thought and changed my wish. Instead, I wished we were both at a different place in our lives, physically and emotionally, so we weren't constrained to just one night. If I lived in the city, maybe we could become friends. And from that friendship, maybe we'd develop into something more.

But that wasn't a possibility in our real lives. I lived over a hundred miles away and rarely came into the city. Watching him ignore me from across the room was truly the last time I'd ever see him outside of my memories.

Feeling even more sick to my stomach over the loss of something I never had, I headed back to the hotel. I still had two more days of the conference before it was time to drive back home and say goodbye to the ghost of the best lover of my life in my rented bed.

When I entered the lobby of the hotel, I was careful to keep my head down and my eyes averted from the glass wall that looked into the bar. I couldn't risk catching Lane's eye one more time and then watching as he completely dismissed me as if I was already a forgotten notch in his belt.

I needed to focus on the good memory of my time with him, not how I was feeling at that moment. The overwhelming sadness and rejection that made me want to jump in my car and drive straight home so I'd never have to face that kind of humiliation again.

10

———

LANE

I was just walking in from the stockroom when I saw Cory enter the lobby through the front door and shuffle in toward the elevators. His coat collar was turned up around his neck and he stared at his feet as if he were trying to avoid being noticed.

Was he trying to avoid being noticed by me?

If I were the reason he looked so...broken, I'd hate myself. But I wasn't so narcissistic to believe that. He was a grown man who knew what he was signing up for when we met. And the fact that he hadn't gone out of his way to ask for a drink from me made me feel better about his current state. He wasn't obsessed with me.

If anyone was obsessed, I was being a little stalkerish by constantly looking for him.

He might have been a little hurt, or more likely pissed, that I didn't smile or wave when we made eye contact, but he knew the score and probably had better things to worry about than me. The weight on his shoulders as he hurried to his room was likely from a situation he was dealing with relating to work or the conference. Or maybe things had been awkward with the colleague he'd hit on the night before. Hopefully they were both mature enough to move past a little drunken flirting so they could go back to the friendship it seemed they had started the evening with when I was watching them together.

A small part of me wanted to follow him up to his room to make sure everything was okay. If he wasn't feeling well, I could ask the concierge to pick up some medicine or get a car to take him to the nearest urgent care.

But then I remembered my rules and came to my senses. He wasn't a lost child or an injured puppy. He was an adult who was perfectly capable of taking care of himself. He'd be fine.

I put the bottles I'd retrieved from storage onto the

shelves on the wall then turned to Jaxon. "Did I miss anything?"

"Nah." He shook his head then did a double take as he looked at me more closely. "Dude, are you feeling okay? You look a little pale."

I swiped my forearm across my brow and shrugged. "I'm fine. Just looking forward to this night ending."

"Got someone already lined up?" He shook his head slowly and grinned. "I don't know how you do it. You were gone for like two minutes and you already found your next victim."

"Victim?" I knew he was joking but the word didn't hit me right. "I am totally up front with every person I see. They know what we're doing and what we aren't doing. It's not my fault if feelings get involved."

"What?" Jaxon crossed his arms over his chest and leaned on the counter. "What the hell are you talking about?"

What was I talking about? I had no idea. Nothing was making sense any more. "Nothing, never mind. It's just been a long day."

Jaxon watched me for a minute then turned back to what he'd been doing. "Whatever you say, man."

I wanted that to be true. I wanted my body to accept that whatever I said was how things would be. That if I said I was fine, I was fine. If I said I didn't care that Cory looked so upset, I didn't care. But that wasn't true at all.

It was like my heart had taken over my whole damn being and I was suddenly a slave to how it felt. Which didn't work for me at all.

We closed up early because there weren't any customers and I still hadn't managed to shake the funk I was in.

Jaxon knew better than to push me to talk, but when we turned off the lights and locked up the door, he put his hand on my shoulder and gave me a squeeze. "I don't know what's going on with you, man, but it'll get better. Bad days happen now and then but they always get better." He grinned and nodded toward the potted succulents I was holding. "And now that you've got some babies to take care of, you'll have a whole new level of fulfillment in your life." He chuckled then walked out of the hotel.

I stood in the lobby for a moment, trying to decide if I should head up to room 525 or just go home. I wanted to check on Cory but that would only make things more complicated. We'd probably end up having sex again, and although that would be amazing in the moment, it might make it even harder to say good bye again.

Reluctantly, I turned toward the front doors and headed home, knowing this was the best plan of action for both of us. Whatever affection we thought we felt was obviously fueled by desire and pheromones.

Neither of us needed to get hopped up on either of those again to just walk away after.

From that point forward, I needed to revise my plan to strangers who were on their last day of a trip, not their first. Then the chances of ever seeing them again were clear from the beginning.

And I wouldn't have to face these kinds of feelings of loss ever again.

11

———

CORY

I got through the conference but the experience had changed for me. It wasn't about learning new technology and finding efficiencies in my workday. It was about avoiding Lane until I could go home so I didn't accidentally jump his bones or beg him for his number.

But I managed to maintain my dignity and finally got home in time to meet my mom for her birthday dinner. She liked me to visit at least once a week, and since I missed our standing Sunday brunch date, I was happy to take her to a nice Italian dinner in Carmel so we could catch up.

"This place is lovely, dear." Mom opened the menu and started reading through the options. "But i don't know how I'll pick just one dish. Everything sounds good."

I briefly glanced through my menu but I knew what I was going to order. "Yeah, it's all good, so go ahead and splurge. It's your birthday so you can go wild."

She glanced at me from above her menu. "The fettuccine Alfredo does look delicious. I haven't had that in ages."

"There you have it." I closed my menu and put it down on the table. "This is the age to have it again."

She closed her menu too. "You're right!"

I shrugged. "Usually am."

Mom swatted away my arrogance then clasped her hands together on top of the menu. "So, how was your trip?"

"Fine." I looked away and toyed with the edge of my menu. "Lots of good talks. I learned some stuff and hope to add some new tools at work.

She cocked her head and was about to open her mouth when the server interrupted to take our order. We both placed our orders and I'd hoped to start up a new topic of conversation, preferably about her and not me.

"How was your week, Mom? Did you do that quilting thing you were telling me about?"

She shook her head as she grinned. "Yes, and I will tell you all about it, but first I want you to tell me what went wrong on your trip."

Fuck, I knew she wouldn't let me get away with anything. Ever since I was a kid, she could read me like a damn book. "It was great. Really. Nothing bad."

Her eyes softened and she reached across the table to rest her hand on mine. "Okay, fine. But something did happen that you're not happy about. What is it?"

"I met someone and thought I felt a connection, but since I live here, it would never work out. So, ya know, just a little disappointing. But that's it. Overall, a good trip."

"Okay, but if you do want to talk. You know I'm here for you. For anything."

"I know, Mom. Thanks." She and I had a conversation when I was in high school about the fact that I was gay, but I'd never brought anyone home so I had no idea what she was thinking. I was just happy she was willing to drop it. "So, tell me about those quilts."

***

It was great to spend time with my mom and hear about her life, but I couldn't really focus on her when my mind was back in San Francisco. The old song wasn't too far from the truth. Then again, I guess my heart was back there too. It was a silly crush, and I knew that. My infatuation was based on the fact that he was the first man I had sex with. And although I knew intellectually he wouldn't be the last, it felt like he was the best I'd ever find, and the weight of that loss was extreme.

When I got home, I downloaded one of those hookup apps for men only. I didn't use my real name or my face, but my abs were decent, so after a few hundred crunches, I took a stomach photo and posted my profile.

Within a few minutes, my phone started dinging with messages from guys who were interested in me. It was flattering. And scary. And more than a little intimidating. But flipping through pictures of hot guys, greased abs, and dick shots was kinda fun. For a little while, at least. After that, it just got sad and a little depressing.

Most of the guys who reached out wanted naked pictures of me, and I definitely wasn't on board with that. I'd always been on the shy side and it was hard enough for me to get naked in front of a lover. There was no way I'd strip down for strangers and send permanent evidence of my body over the internet. What if they ended up on a porn site? Or worse, what if my mom ever came across them?

I'd die.

So I played around on the app for another hour and fell asleep on the couch with the TV on in the background. It was no mystery why a man like Lane wanted nothing to do with me. I was practically in love after one night, and I fell asleep to photos of naked stranger dicks instead of making plans to hook up with any of the cocks offered to me.

12

LANE

Two weeks had passed since Cory disappeared from the bar, and I was still in a funk.

At first, I chalked it up to just being busy with work and not being in the mood to hook up with anyone. But after a few days, I still didn't have the same libido I once did. There was just a weird feeling in my belly that made me think any other encounter would be a disappointment. Like I had reached my peak, and it was all downhill from there.

I'd never personally experienced depression, but I started to wonder if maybe that's what I was going through. Maybe it was more than just a cute guy who had gotten under my skin. Maybe the all-consuming obsession with Cory and the night we spent together wasn't about him at all.

Maybe it was about me. I was getting older, and although thirty-five was still several months away, I would be crossing over that threshold sooner rather than later. My anxious discontent might have just been my body telling me it was time to stop with my playboy antics and grow the fuck up.

Or maybe I finally wanted more than just a night with someone. That was a sobering thought that didn't ease my mysterious ache.

I was cleaning up some broken glass on the counter when a familiar face entered my periphery.

"Hey, cowboy. You up for a ride?"

A slow smile spread across my lips as I recognized an old friend. Well, not really a friend, more like a twice yearly fuck buddy. For guys who were spread out with more than a few months in between, I didn't consider them to be a repeat. "Hey, Dustin. When did you get into town?"

He leaned across the counter to give me a kiss on the cheek. "Earlier today. It's just for the one night, but

I'm glad you're working because my trips to the city aren't the same without seeing you." He winked, reminding me of why I'd always been attracted to him.

"Yeah, it's good to see you too. How's everything going?"

"Things are great at home. Mark just made partner, so he's even busier than usual. I think he was as excited for me to get out of town and burn some of my pent-up energy as I was."

I chuckled, not completely understanding their relationship even though it wasn't as uncommon as most people probably thought. Dustin and Mark had been married for years, and were committed for a decade before that, but they both explored outside interests when they were traveling.

At first, it was weird for me to be with a married man, at least one with a husband I'd met and really liked. But those fears were quickly alleviated when Mark himself thanked me for always showing his husband a good time because Dustin came home from his San Francisco trips in a much better mood than when he left.

It was a bit uncomfortable at the time, but to each their own.

I cleared up the last of the glass shards then looked up at Dustin and sighed. "You know I'm always happy to see you, and you're one of my favorite out of town guests." I gave him a sincere smile to let him know I was being serious. "But I've kind of been going through this weird thing lately. I'm just not in the mood tonight."

Dustin's jaw dropped, and it was obvious he was in as much shock over my words as I felt for having said them. "No." He shook his head and put his hands on his hips. "No way. Whatever you're going through can wait until I'm out of here tomorrow. Tonight, you're with me." He pulled a plastic room key out of his pocket and slid it across the counter. "What time are you gonna get out of here?"

I looked at my watch. "About an hour."

"Perfect. I'll go get cleaned up, and I'll see you then."

———

THAT WEIRD FEELING in my belly only got stronger after Dustin left me with his key. The best medicine was probably to just spend the night with Dustin and try to get Cory out of my system completely. Dustin and I had strong chemistry together and always had a great time, but it was never like the connection and synchronization I'd felt with Cory.

I'd never felt that with anyone. Not even Jake.

My usual rush to get the bar locked up was absent as I found myself stalling. I was horny as fuck and Dustin would scratch that itch beautifully. But I just couldn't make myself do it. I couldn't dredge up the desire to go for it. I wanted to make it happen, and I gave it the old college try. But even after trudging all the way up his room and standing outside his door for a good five minutes, I wasn't able to go in.

I put the key on the floor and quietly slid it under the door, far enough inside that no one passing by would be able to grab it, but not so far that Dustin might see it and come after me. When I was sure he hadn't noticed the key, I left the hotel, eager to get home for the night and wash away yet another lonely day.

13

CORY

I'D BEEN WORKING AT HOME MORE OFTEN SINCE the conference. Things were fine between me and Jasmine, but I still felt awkward about my unsuccessful seduction so I needed some time to pass before really spending a lot of time with her. Besides, I was also grieving over Lane and what my life could have been like if things had ended differently, and I needed alone time to wallow in that pain.

But Jasmine wouldn't have it.

She let me have a few weeks to lick my wounds and avoid the embarrassment of having to face her but then she cornered me and dragged me out to lunch. We went to a deli near the office that had the most amazing pastrami sandwiches.

Jasmine and I both ordered the same thing before she crossed her arms over her chest and looked at me from across the table. "Please tell me this isn't about me."

"What?" I crossed my arms over my chest too, mimicking her behavior. "What are you talking about?"

"You!" She threw her arms out and then rested her elbows on the table. "You've been avoiding me since San Francisco and I don't want there to be this weirdness between us. I miss you."

"Oh." I relaxed my arms too, slumping forward a little bit. "No, sorry. It's not about you. Well, not all about you."

She seemed relieved but then narrowed her gaze. "Then what is it?"

I didn't want to get into it with her, but I needed to talk to someone...who wasn't my mother. "First of all, I'd like to apologize for hitting on you. I shouldn't have done that, and I'm glad you said no. That would have been a mistake."

She shrugged, agreeing without having hurt feelings for being called a mistake. "No need to apologize. It's water under the bridge. So what else ya got?"

I closed my eyes and threw my head back, not wanting to face her when I came out to her. "I met a guy."

For the first time ever, Jasmine was speechless.

When she didn't say anything, I opened my eyes and peeked at her. "Are you surprised?"

She looked at me for another minute and then smiled. "Actually, no. That makes more sense than you and me...so I guess I'm not surprised at all."

I rolled my eyes but felt some relief that she wasn't upset or appalled so far. "Well, anyway, we spent the night together and it was great."

Now her whole disposition changed and her eyes sparkled with excitement. "Oohhh, good for you! What did he look like? Was he hot? Was it that cute redhead CEO dude we were talking to at lunch?"

"No, no." I paused for a moment while the server put our drinks and sandwiches in front of us. "It was the bartender, he—"

"That gorgeous dude with the tatts in the hotel bar?"

I smiled. "Yeah, his name is Lane."

She whistled and picked up her sandwich. "You've got good taste, Cor."

That made me chuckle, and I already felt better. "Well, the thing is...it was my first time with a guy."

Her eyes got wide. "Seriously? Like first, first?"

I nodded. "I've always known I was interested in men but I was afraid...and then suddenly he was offering and I was accepting and..."

"And what?" She smacked the table in front of her. "What? You're killing me!"

"And, it was amazing..." I sighed and leaned back, not bothering to touch my food. "Really amazing."

She held her hands up. "So, you're dating him now? Is that what's kept you so busy lately?"

My smile dropped and I had to say the words out loud that had been on repeat in my head for weeks. "No, I was just a one-night thing for him. He didn't even say hi to me the next day when I saw him in the bar."

She reached across the table and placed her manicured hand on my forearm. "Oh, honey. I'm sorry."

"No, it's fine." I shrugged and tried to play off my pain as nonchalance. "I knew what I was signing up for when we went to my room. I just didn't expect him to be burned into my brain so permanently. I figured he'd just be a fun memory but I can't think about anything else. He's like an obsession or something."

She inhaled a deep breath and looked at me with sympathy in her eyes. "My first love was like that too." She held up her palm to silence my objection to her words. "I know you're not in love. I'm just saying, I thought I was in love with the first guy I slept with and he was the only thing I could think about for almost a year. But I was just a notch for him and after a while I came to accept that. It wasn't easy or fast, but it did happen."

"I know it will. And I'm sorry you thought it was you." I patted her hand that was still on my arm. "I've missed you too."

We both felt better enough to find our appetites so we dug into our sandwiches over our usual banter.

And then Jasmine had to throw another curveball at me. "Oh my god!"

I startled, looking around to see what the matter was but there was nothing out of the ordinary. "What?"

"You should go out with Brayden. He's perfect for you."

I furrowed my brow, trying to place the name. "Is that the guy in sales?"

"No, you're thinking of Brandon. Also cute but not gay." She stood up and we both started walking toward the exit. "Brayden is in Accounting. He's single and goes out all the time. If nothing else, he can introduce you to other guys and show you the clubs and stuff."

We walked out to the street and headed back to the office. "Yeah, I guess I could stand to meet a few people. A guy can't have too many friends, right?"

14

LANE

I HADN'T GONE MORE THAN A WEEK WITHOUT SEX since high school.

As the three-week mark came and went, I started to get worried that maybe I'd never get my sex drive back. Maybe Cory was my destiny, and instead of grasping that gift when he was presented to me, I ignored him, flipping off the universe and subjecting myself to a life of sexless solitude.

When Jaxon cornered me about it at work, I finally came clean. Admitting I'd probably made a mistake about the rest of my life was painful, but I reasoned that the sooner I accepted my fate, the easier it would be to embrace it.

"So, that's it. I'm not suicidal. I'm not on the brink of a melt down." I slipped my hands in my pocket and leaned against the bar. "I'm just...destined to be alone. Monk-like, if you will."

Jaxon rolled his eyes at my dramatics and then reached for my phone from where it was hiding under the counter. "What's his name?"

"Cory, why?" I reached for my phone, but Jaxon twisted away from me so I couldn't reach his hand as he ignored me and began tapping at the screen.

"I'm not finding a Cory in here." He glanced at me impatiently. "What name is he listed under?"

"Dude, did you listen to me at all?" I grabbed my phone from his hands and slipped it into my back pocket. "I don't have his number. I wouldn't even have his first name if he didn't insist on getting mine."

Jaxon winced as if I'd personally offended him. "Dude, that's cold. You don't even ask for names?"

I shrugged. "Not usually. It's easier to keep my distance if they're just nameless memories."

He scoffed. "Well, that didn't work for you, did it?"

"I don't know what to do." I shook my head, pissed that I was even having this conversation but even more pissed that it wasn't helping to resolve anything. Nothing would resolve this because I'd dug my own grave this time. "I'll never see him again so it doesn't really matter. I need to move on or get over him or something."

Lane held out his hand then pointed to my phone. "Yeah, that's what I was trying to do."

"What the hell does that mean?"

"Get his number from the lobby and call him. Maybe he's coming back to town in a few months and you can have something to look forward to. That might help."

I didn't think it would help because I didn't think Cory would forgive me. I was a total dick to him when he was in the bar last time. I could have at least smiled or waved, but I was afraid of leading him on. Clingy guys aren't sexy at all. And there I was being even worse than a clingy guy.

I was being a stalker psycho.

"That's illegal. They won't just give me his number."

Jaxon rolled his eyes again and then walked around the counter. "When was he here?"

I shouldn't have had the date on the tip of my tongue but it rolled off smoothly. "September 12th."

"Give me a minute. I doubt there was more than one Cory here that night."

Before I could argue, Jaxon disappeared and I was left with a new feeling in my belly. This was more like hope. I still felt off, but now there was a twinge of anticipation that made me think Jaxon might be onto something. If he could actually get Cory's number for me, then at least I'd have an option. An option I might never take, but having it was better than what I had now, which was a big ol' pile of nothing.

Maybe Cory would hang up on me. Maybe he'd tell me off and block me from ever calling him again. Or maybe he'd say yes. I wasn't exactly sure what the question would be, but if I did ask him for something, maybe he'd say yes and we could explore things through a new lens.

A lens that wasn't just made for short-range views. Something meant to go the distance.

And maybe I'd find the view was different from the other side of the fence. The side where happy couples lived together day and night, not just a few times a year when the company was footing the bill.

It was a lot to hope for, but when Jaxon finally came back with a big grin on his face, I knew there could be more for me...if I wasn't too chicken shit to ask for it.

15

——

CORY

Brayden was a good-looking guy. More clean cut and preppy than Lane, but in a really nice way. I agreed to have dinner with him on Friday because I needed to do something to take my mind off Lane and to at least try to move on.

I wasn't sure if Brayden would be a potential love connection, but he was a starting point. And as long as I kept meeting new people and taking new chances, there was hope of finding someone who wanted me as much as I wanted them. At least that's what all those Hallmark movies led me to believe.

I met him at the restaurant because we were keeping things casual. I didn't want to be obligated to stay if things went south, and I didn't want to get stuck bar hopping if that's where he wanted to take the night. The restaurant was busy but on the outskirts of town and mostly visited by locals. My place was closer to the tourist areas so I was used to restaurants being jam-packed with people taking selfies with their food and loud families toting exhausted babies through all the landmarks.

"This place is nice." I sat in the chair facing the front door, close to the window so we could watch passersby as they headed home for the weekend or out for the night. "I've never been here before."

Brayden sat down across from me and placed his phone on the table, facing up. "Yeah, I like it because the food is delicious but I can usually get a table without much of a wait. Win/win."

"Definitely." I opened my menu and immediately was drawn to the porcini risotto. "Oh, they have my favorite!"

"Yeah?" Brayden closed his menu and clasped his hands on top of it, politely giving me his entire focus. "What's that?"

"Porcini risotto. My mom makes it now and then but whenever I see it on a menu, I usually get it."

"Good choice. It's delicious." He opened the wine menu. "Are you white or red?"

I grinned at his casual conversation. "Usually white, but I can do red if you want to get a bottle."

He nodded. "I like how you think, but white is good. They have a nice Pinot Gris from Noble Vines if you like local vintners."

"Sounds good." Truthfully, I wasn't well-versed on wines. I liked most whites and could stomach most reds as long as they weren't too syrupy, but that was the extent of my wine sophistication. "Whatever you like is fine with me."

We ordered a bottle at the same time that we ordered our entrees then had to start the small talk. Fortunately, Brayden didn't ever seem to be at a loss of topics. And there was never a lull in the conversation. We talked about Jasmine and how we both knew her. Then we talked about our jobs.

And finally, my recent sexual awakening came up.

"Jasmine said you're pretty new to all this." He took a sip of his wine as he looked at me over the glass.

I scoffed. "Yeah, did she also tell you she turned down my half-drunken offer for a hookup and then I ended up with a bartender at the hotel we were staying at?"

He laughed. "Nice work, kid. No, she didn't go into that level of detail but I'm impressed. A hotel hookup is usually reserved for a more experienced player. Good for you!"

My smile dropped and I leaned back in the seat. "Not really. I kinda fell for the guy and he didn't want anything to do with me after that."

Brayden was quiet as he waited for me to continue.

"Sorry, I guess that's not really okay to say when I'm having dinner with someone else." I was an idiot. And an asshole.

"Don't worry about it." He reached across the table and patted my hand briefly. "I can tell your heart isn't ready to move on yet, so if you want to talk about this guy, that's cool. I'm a good listener."

I didn't want to talk about Lane, but I figured Brayden might have a unique perspective and could offer me some hope that I would get over Lane...eventually. "I feel like a sixteen year old who is in love with the guy who popped his cherry. It's so stupid but I just can't stop thinking about it."

Brayden didn't seem annoyed by my admission. If anything, he seemed sympathetic to my plight. "I've been there. We've all been there at some point. I wish I could say it's gonna be an easy journey, but it usually isn't."

I rolled my eyes and chuckled. "Thanks, that makes me feel so much better."

"Sorry." He smiled before imparting his sage wisdom. "But it will get better. The more you get out and meet new people, the more his memory will fade and you'll make room for new memories."

"Yeah, I know." I sighed heavily then finished the wine in my glass. "And I appreciate you letting me pour my heart out. If you ever want to go out again, I promise to be a better companion."

"You're a great companion, Cory." His eyes were kind and I could feel his sincerity. "And that guy was an idiot to let you get away."

We left the restaurant with a handshake and then a hug before I got in my car and drove home. I really liked Brayden as a friend, but he was nothing like Lane. And now that I'd had a taste of a man like Lane, I couldn't settle for anything less. Which was depressing all over again.

When I got home, I took a quick shower then hopped into bed. I put on a t-shirt to ward off the chill in the air, but I didn't put on anything else. Instead of going straight to sleep, I grabbed my phone and tried out that hookup app again. I wasn't looking for an actual hookup, but it was the most concentrated collection of porn I'd ever come across so I started flipping through photos as I laid on my sheets with my fist around my dick.

It took a few minutes to get into it, but after a while, I was hard and getting closer to completion with all the photos of guys with huge muscles and sexy tattoos. I was almost there, almost ready to let myself run with the fantasy in my head when the phone rang in my hand.

I was startled by the sound and the phone slipped out of my hand and off the bed. "Shit!"

Instinctively, I chased after it, getting down on all fours to reach for it between my bed frame and the night stand.

16

─────

LANE

I'd been staring at my phone for an hour with his number typed in and only the send button between me and a conversation with Cory. It was late on Friday night and probably not the best time to make a surprise call, but I got off work early and had a few shots in my belly so my judgment wasn't at its peak.

And using Facetime to make the call was completely a whim.

What I didn't expect to see was Cory's naked body and then the underside of his mattress while he reached for the phone he'd apparently dropped.

He must not have been paying attention because he put the phone to his ear to speak, but he was holding it upside down so the camera was aimed down, right at his hard cock as his fingers lightly wrapped around it and rubbed, keeping it hard while he took the call. "Hello."

"Hi, is this Cory?" I knew it was by the shape of that perfect cock. I'd be able to pick it out of a lineup even though I'd only spent a few hours with it.

"Yeah, who's this?" His fingers stopped moving but his dick seemed to grow even thicker.

"It's Lane, from the hotel in San Francisco." I cleared my throat, wondering when the right time was to tell him I could see him.

The camera swept up as if he'd moved his head back and then he laid back on the bed. "Uh, right. Lane. Hi."

"Hi." I chuckled to myself at his forced nonchalance. He was adorable. When his fist started moving in full strokes, I knew I had to tell him the truth. "Actually, we're on Facetime so you might want to adjust the camera."

Cory's face immediately appeared in the camera and he stared at me for a long moment before looking down at his hand. "Oh fuck."

I smiled. "It's okay. I obviously caught you at a bad time. Do you want me to call back?"

His eyes were wide but he held his right hand in front of the screen. "I'll stop. I promise."

"Don't stop on my account." I shook my head and grinned. "That was fucking sexy."

His cheeks flushed and I could imagine his whole body was burning with embarrassment. "Sorry."

"I'm not."

He looked at me for a few minutes before gathering his thoughts. "Wait, why are you calling? How did you even get my number."

This is where I was either going to win him over or scare him off. It could easily go either way, but I was too deep into this dumb idea to change my mind. I had to just go for it and lay my cards on the table. "Well, I got your number from a friend at the hotel. I'm sorry, I know that's a little creepy, but I've been thinking about you since you left town, and I just wanted to say hi."

His brows furrowed and his jaw relaxed as if he had something to say but then he stayed silent, clearly confused by what I was saying.

"First, let me apologize for ignoring you when you came back to the bar the next night. That was a shitty thing to do and I've regretted it ever since."

"You have?" He turned on his side and propped the phone against a pillow so he didn't have to hold the phone. "I figured you thought I was being clingy and you didn't want to ever see me again."

I inhaled a deep breath then slowly blew it out. "Yeah, that wasn't entirely untrue. I mean, that's my usual move and that's what I thought I wanted." I looked into his eyes to make sure he was hearing me. "But you've stuck with me in a way no one else ever has."

He gave me a half smile and his eyes almost glowed. "Yeah, I know what you mean."

"You do?" I laid back in my bed and propped my phone up similar to how his was. "You've thought about me too?"

"Every day." He looked away for a moment as he confessed his true feelings. "I've been telling myself it's just because you're my first...but I can't stop thinking about you and that night." He looked back at me. "It was really amazing. I had no idea it could be that good."

I nodded. "I didn't know that either. It was different with you...and that's why I had to call."

He swallowed hard and I could see the anticipation building in his eyes.

I hated to get his hopes up when I had no idea where things would go, but I couldn't walk away from him without at least trying. "I was wondering if you'd want to go to dinner with me if I went down to Monterey. Maybe tomorrow night?"

The worry on his face dissolved as a big smile lifted his cheeks. "Seriously? You're gonna come here to see me?"

I shrugged. "If that's okay with you. I can't promise anything because I've never done anything like this before, but I think we owe it to ourselves to at least have one dinner to see how things go."

Cory nodded as he agreed. "I'd love to have dinner with you, Lane. Tomorrow would be great."

17

CORY

As soon as I woke up Saturday morning, I called Jasmine to tell her about my dinner with Brayden, and more importantly, my call with Lane. She was thrilled with both stories and insisted on taking me shopping to get a perfect outfit for my first real date with a man. I was glad for her help because my wardrobe was more casual Friday than dinner date with a sexy man, so I needed all the help I could get.

We hit one of the high-end shopping areas, and I tried on slim cut slacks that I wasn't sure I'd be able to sit in and sweaters that cost more than my computer. But in the end, we found a nice outfit for dinner and a few extra shirts to keep on hand in case he decided to stay for the weekend. I wanted him to at least spend the night, but I had no idea what the protocols were in these situations so I was just going to play it by ear.

He was taking the risk by coming to see me, so I didn't want to overwhelm him with questions or decisions or declarations. I was just excited to see him again and hopefully feel those strong muscles under my fingertips, preferably while we were both naked and he was plowing into me.

The time went fast and slow at the same time. When I got the text from Lane saying he was twenty minutes out, I brushed my teeth for the fourth time and made another round through my little bungalow to make sure nothing was out of place. I was a bit of a minimalist so there wasn't ever clutter, but I didn't want a speck of dust or a dirty dish to give Lane the wrong impression about me. I had no idea what kind of impression he already had, but it was good enough that he was driving for two hours to have dinner with me.

As long as I didn't do anything really stupid, I might get lucky again.

I did something stupid.

I should have known I would. I'm just too much of a dork to play it smooth, so when Lane knocked at my door, I practically jumped into his arms. My plan was to invite him in, offer him a drink and feel him out a bit. But that didn't quite work out because he looked so damn good in that tight shirt and ripped jeans that my knees got weak and I couldn't help but throw myself at him.

He wrapped those thick arms around my back and held me to his chest, sighing against my temple as if he was as eager to feel me in his arms as I was to be there. I didn't want to let him go, but when I felt my eyes begin to moisten, I realized I needed to rein it in a bit. I was overplaying my hand hard, and if I wanted any chance of a normal evening with him, I needed to give him some space to breathe.

I pulled out of his arms and then waved him inside my small home. "Come in, please."

He walked inside and took a look around. "You live here alone?"

"Yeah." I closed the door and walked toward the kitchen. "Can I get you something to drink? Do you need to use the bathroom or anything?"

He shook his head. "No, I'm fine. This place is great. I forget what normal homes look like after living in a tiny apartment in the city with a slob for a roommate."

Grateful I'd taken the extra time to make my house spotless, I motioned toward the sofa. "Well, have a seat. I'm sure you're tired from the long drive."

He was bolder than I could ever be, so it wasn't shocking when he reached for my hand and gently tugged me toward the sofa so we could both sit down together. There was some space between us, but only a few inches.

"You look good." He fingered the trim of my sleeve as he felt the fabric. "I like this shirt."

"Thanks." I cleared my throat and looked down at his fingers, wishing they'd explore farther. "My friend Jasmine helped me pick it out."

He grinned. "The woman from the conference?"

"Yeah." I reached across the back of the sofa and placed my hand near Lane's shoulder. I desperately wanted to touch him but I didn't want to be too forward. Not yet, at least. "She knows about you and how I've been a little off since I got home."

"You too?" Lane lowered his hand and placed it on my thigh. "I thought I was having some kind of low-key panic attack or some other kind of medical episode. I finally realized it was much more complicated than that."

"Complicated?" I could feel the frown form on my face but I didn't want to seem whiny so I tried to school my features into curiosity. "How so?"

"Well, for one, I didn't have any way to reach you. And I had no idea where in the world you lived. If I didn't have connections in the hotel who were willing to break some white-collar laws, I would have never been able to find you." He raised an eyebrow and gave me a playful look. "And it doesn't seem like you were planning to find me again anytime soon."

Now it was my turn to raise an eyebrow. "I did that once and you turned me away. No, I didn't plan to do that again."

He sighed and reached for the hand in my lap, holding it between both of his. "I'm sorry about that, Cory. I was stupid but I want to make it up to you. If you'll let me."

I nodded, not having any words to respond verbally.

He stared into my eyes before leaning forward and pressing his lips to mine, kissing me softly in a way I'd never been kissed before.

18

LANE

When I was finally able to taste Cory on my lips, I felt like I could breathe. I didn't understand the intense connection between us but I was done fighting it. I wanted to embrace it and nurture it and let it grow to whatever it was supposed to be.

At first, our kisses were soft and gentle, but they quickly turned hungry. I leaned across the sofa and covered his body with mine, exploring his mouth with my tongue while my hands explored his body—first over his clothes and then below as I quickly divested him of the stylish clothes he'd picked out for me.

The fact that he went out of his way to wear something nice for me made me even more hopeful that his feelings for me were as strong as mine were for him. As I was trying to get his pants off, he smiled and pressed his hand to my chest. "Want to go to the bedroom?"

"Definitely." I stood up in a fluid motion with Cory in my arms. "Lead the way."

While we walked, I toed off my shoes and pulled my shirt over my head, not wanting to waste any time once we got to his room. Before I took off my jeans, I pulled a few condoms out of one pocket then a few packets of lube from the other. Cory probably had supplies on hand, but then again, since this was new to him, he might not have had what we needed, and I didn't want a trip to the drug store to slow down getting inside him again.

I watched with my breath held as Cory slipped out of his slacks and lay on his bed, offering himself to me in much the same way he did in his hotel room. I lowered my jeans and my naked cock jutted out in front of me, pointing to Cory's opening as if it were a divining rod. In some ways it was because it knew where I needed to go to find my happiness.

Before giving in to my own needs, I dropped to my knees and leaned over the side of the bed so I could take Cory's cock in my mouth. This time, I didn't stop when he got close to coming. I sucked his smooth skin between my lips and licked and sucked with all my best techniques, showing him exactly what he could expect if he were to give me a chance to do this again. And again. And again.

Cory bucked his hips beneath me, gripping his comforter while trying to hold back the desperate sounds escaping from his throat. "God, Lane. I'm gonna come."

I sucked harder, wanting to taste it all as I gently fingered his hole to loosen him up. I didn't bother with the lube yet because there was enough wetness dripping down into him that my finger easily slipped in without any resistance. As soon as I was knuckle deep, Cory blew his load, coming hard against the mattress while shooting thick cream down my throat. I continued to suck, breathing through my nose so not a drop was lost while he rode out the waves of his orgasm.

By the time the tension of his muscles relaxed and he was catching his breath, I knew we were both ready for more. I gently removed my finger from his ass and reached for the supplies to get suited up.

Before I could open the packets, Cory sat up. "Was that okay?"

I smiled and ripped open the condom wrapper. "I thought it was pretty awesome. Was it okay for you?"

He smiled. "Not that. That was definitely awesome. I mean, the fact that I came in your mouth. Was that okay."

I secured the rubber in place then reached for some lube before leaning over Cory until he was laying back again. "It was perfect. Anything that feels good to you is always okay. Got it?"

He nodded and watched my hands work the lube up and down my shaft before slipping under his ass. "Got it."

"So, now we get to what we're really good at." I angled my hips so my cock was aimed straight for his hole. "Are you ready."

"I'm so fucking ready, Lane. I've been ready for weeks." He gripped my shoulders with both hands and dug his fingers into my tight muscles. "Fuck me."

I held in a groan as I slowly pushed through his opening and kept going until I was fully seated inside Cory's channel. He was hot and tight and I wanted to come just from the pressure surrounding my dick. But I held my breath and waited out the intensity for a few moments until we were both ready to keep going. "I'm going to fuck you this time, Cory. And then after that, I'm going to show you what it's like to make love."

As promised, I fucked him hard and fast, driving him to another climax just seconds before I reached my own.

And although I'd never really made love to someone before, I felt like that was where we were heading. And if there was any person in the world for me to do it with, Cory seemed like the only choice. The only man to affect me in a way that changed my entire lifestyle and made me want to be a better man.

The kind of man who deserved a man like Cory.

19

———

CORY

WE SKIPPED DINNER ON SATURDAY, CHOOSING TO stay in bed and experiment with different ways of pleasing each other. But when we woke up on Sunday morning, we were both starving. I had ingredients to make breakfast, but neither of us wanted to be stuck in the kitchen so we decided to take a walk and pick up coffee and bagels from a local cafe. It was a beautiful day and the warm sun felt good on my skin. Not as good as the flush of heat that flooded through me every time Lane touched me, but it was nice to get some fresh air and stretch our legs.

We sat outside the cafe with our breakfast and watched the waves break on the other side of the pier. "When do you have to leave?"

Lane shrugged. "I'm off work tonight so I don't have to rush back."

My eyes widened and a grin broke across my face. "So you can stay tonight too?"

He chuckled. "Yeah, if you'd like me to."

"Of course, I'd like you to!" I grabbed his hand and held it on the table. "I'd ask you to stay forever if that didn't seem weird or creepy."

Lane cocked his head and looked into my eyes. "It wouldn't be any more weird or creepy than me stealing your contact information and coming down here to visit you."

I wanted to keep looking into those dreamy eyes, but I didn't know how to respond. I didn't know how he wanted me to respond. "I'm so glad you came."

He nodded. "Me too."

"And if you wanted to stay, I'd let you. Yes, it's probably ridiculous, and we might drive each other crazy after a week or two...but if you wanted to try that...either now or at some point in the future, I'd be all in." I shrugged and considered my words. "I guess I don't know how relationships are supposed to go, or if that's even what you want, but I do know that I want you to stay forever. I might not always feel that way, and you might not feel that way now or in the future, that's what I feel now. So, just putting that out there."

"I can't just quit my job, but I do have a few weeks of vacation time saved up." He pulled my hand to his lips and kissed it. "I'd have to go home to take care of some stuff, but if you're serious, I'd be up for spending a week or two with you to see how things go. LIke you said, maybe we'll be over each other after that."

I frowned at that thought but Lane reached for the corner of my lip and lifted it up.

"Yeah, I don't think that'll happen either."

"What do you think will happen?" I whispered, nervous to hear his honest answer.

"I'll fall even deeper for you." He squeezed my hand, holding my gaze.

I swallowed the emotion in my throat and nodded. "I'm not sure it's possible for me to fall any deeper, but I'm looking forward to trying."

IT WAS A WHIRLWIND ROMANCE, if that's what you could even call it. We'd barely met and were already totally obsessed with each other. It didn't seem like a traditional love story, at least none of those I'd heard from friends or even seen in movies. But it seemed like the right story for us. I didn't know if our future was predestined or if we just happened to be in the right place at the right time...with the right needs.

But whatever circumstances brought us together, we were both committed to following through to see where we would end up. I imagined we'd grow old together with adopted children and grandchildren surrounding us until the end of our days. Or maybe we'd have a natural ending at some point to a beautiful love story.

Either way, Lane was my first and only love. And according to him, I was his.

And that was what we both needed. Now and forever.

Ready to go darker?

Turn the page for a sneak peek at the series:

Twelve for Two Hundred

Men of the Vault #1

20

CHAPTER 1: EDGE

As soon as I step inside the smoke-filled warehouse, I regret my decision to come. It's been over a month since I've stopped by, but the last few visits have done more harm than good.

Coming to The Vault used to be an occasional indulgence I appreciated. I'd drop a few grand and spend an hour with a guy eager to please me in any way I wanted. That was usually just a blow job and a fuck, in that order. But some of the guys are more frisky and would offer more.

I haven't accepted the more extreme offers, but when someone is begging you to choke them while they come or truss them up before fucking, it can be hard to say no.

I'm not too proud to admit that I'm less kinky than some of my buddies who come here. I don't get off on the violent shit they like. If I leave a guy bleeding, I prefer it be from bite marks on the back of his shoulder. And if his ass is tender, I want it to be from the pounding I gave it, not from being fucked with a wire brush or caned to within an inch of his life.

But when someone asks for it rough, I can't exactly deny them. Stupid shit like that can get a person killed. In my world, mercy is for the meek, and the meek don't deserve to live.

But what gets other people off isn't my business. Every member of Rod Tanner's stable has a very clear idea of what he's signing up for when he joins. Tanner gives them a contract for two hundred thousand dollars in exchange for twelve months of their complete and total servitude.

Anything goes during those twelve months.

"Edge, my man. It's been too long." Asher is working the lobby tonight and pulls me into a half hug.

"Yeah, been busy." I pat his back then step out of his reach. "You know how it is."

"Oh, I know." Asher laughs. "But there're some things you just gotta make time for."

I grunt and hand over my credit card. My business associates know better than to accept cash from me. At least not at face value. Although, when I'm selling it to them at twenty-five cents on the dollar, they're more than eager to fill their pockets with my product.

"Anyone new?" I tap my finger on the counter, anxious to get inside. I just need to get this itch scratched so I can get the hell out of here.

"Always." Asher slides my card across the counter then hands me a receipt for Vault Consultants. That's the front Tanner uses for his less-than-legal enterprises. At least this one. I don't know all of his businesses, and I don't want to. The less blood on my hands, the better. "In fact, we got a new batch of interns starting tonight. Definitely a few gems in there. You'll have a good time."

I nod as I turn toward the door. After my fingerprint scan is accepted, the light on the entry panel flashes green and the door unlocks. "Have a good one, Ash."

Smoke and steam fill my lungs as I walk into the dimly lit room. Tanner keeps the humidity levels high so his clients have an incentive to get in and get out quickly. No hanging around to cuddle. The added visual of seeing a thin sheen of sweat glistening off the hard bodies on display is just gravy.

Glass boxes are set on pedestals in the center of the large warehouse. Inside each three foot by three foot enclosure is a naked man sitting on a wooden stool. This process always makes me feel a little dirty. It's not because I feel guilt. I don't. But seeing these guys dressed in tight jeans and a snug t-shirt would be ten times sexier to me than just shopping amongst the flesh.

Instead of appraising the bodies of each man I pass, my gaze locks on to each of theirs. I want to see life in their eyes. Interest. Too many of the guys on display are lifeless shells. Drones to their physical instincts without mental or emotional awareness. It's easy to walk past those without a second glance.

Just as I'm starting to feel frustrated at the offerings, I catch a glimpse of red peeking around the hip of one man. His eyes are perusing my body, and he flinches when they meet mine. With just a slight change in posture, I can see his entire body tense up as I approach his cage and take a closer look.

The tattoo that initially caught my attention is a surprise. Not just because it's only worn by members of the Nicola family but because no one in the Nicola family has been seen in the state in over five years. That family was run out of town after messing with the wrong cartel.

If this guy is actually Nicola, Tanner is going to be in a world of hurt once they find out where he is. The only way to know for sure is to get a closer look at the small tattoo of a lion holding a bloody lamp from his jaw. In the swirling lines of golden mane is a coded serial number describing the person's lineage. Even from the other side of the glass and with a foot of dim, muggy space separating us, I can clearly see the encrypted number.

He's one of them.

21

CHAPTER 2: LIAM

The hair on the back of my neck is standing straight up as the man in black jeans and a black leather jacket circles me. His gaze is heavy on my skin as he inspects every inch of bare flesh I have on offer. I've spent the past two weeks practicing my stamina and technique with three of Tanner's trainers, but nothing has prepared me for this moment.

Being on display like an animal has made me question my sanity for the past hour. The money is good. Great even. But now that I'm here and strangers are practically holding up rulers as if they're measuring for window coverings, I want to pull the plug. I want to beg Tanner to tear up our contract and let me leave with my dignity.

But that isn't possible. Even if he was willing to let me leave, which he made very clear would not be an option once the contract was signed, I will never have my dignity. I lost that a long time ago. Long before I ever heard about Rod Tanner and The Vault.

I thought I could handle it. I thought I was tough enough. But every time I glance down at the man just a few inches away from the thick glass walls, I realize I'm not tough at all. I'm a goddamn pussy, just like my uncle has been saying for the past ten years. Ever since my parents were killed by a car bomb, and I was taken in by my dad's brother.

Without realizing what I'm doing, my open palm drifts to my left hip and covers the tattoo there.

The tattoo I begged my uncle not to mar my body with.

The tattoo that represents everything I hate.

Everyone I hate.

I practically jump out of my skin when a low thumping sound on the glass catches my attention. When I look up into those hazel eyes, my breath catches, and I have to force my eyes to stay open and on him. I've been trained to not speak unless spoken to, to never challenge authority.

And this man is dripping with authority.

Even through the glass partition, I can feel the power radiating off him. He looks like he's about to reach for the tag on the door when another man places a hand on his shoulder.

Their interaction is brief, but I don't miss the way his eyes harden as they bounce between me and the new man. And before I realize what's happened, the man with the hazel eyes is walking away, and I'm being pulled in the arms of the stranger with an evil smile.

"AM I YOUR FIRST?" The door to the private bedroom isn't even completely closed before the man starts yanking off his shirt. He's wearing a dark blue button down that would be commonplace in any office building. But in this moist and dank room, it just looks uncomfortable.

"My first?" I want to cover myself with the pillow but modesty isn't allowed. There are three rules

Tanner insisted we agree to before we signed on the dotted line.

1. *No* is not an option.
2. Modesty will not be tolerated.
3. A willing and pleasant attitude is expected at all times.

In return, he promises to release me at the end of my twelve month contract with no lasting physical damage. That seemed adequate at the time I agreed to it. But now, I realize the emotional damage will be immeasurable.

"Yeah. Tanner said you guys are new." He rips the shirt over his head then starts toeing off his shoes. "Am I your first?"

"Uh, yeah." I force a smile, remembering I'm supposed to be enjoying this. "Is that okay?"

The man stops in the middle of yanking his socks off with his pants. "Fuck yeah. I love breaking in the newbies."

I don't know how to react to that. Is he being funny? Will he be gentle? Does he like pain?

I don't have to wonder for long because as soon he's naked, he walks to the small dresser next to the bed and opens up the bottom drawer. The scary drawer. The drawer with the tools that were never intended to be inserted inside a human body.

Order Now

www.ingramcontent.com/pod-product-compliance
Lightning Source LLC
Chambersburg PA
CBHW051424150726
48000CB00005B/1948